Diary of a Diva's Daughter
with a
DO-IT-ALL DAD
Starring
Brave Rave

Diary of a Diva's Daughter
with a Do-It-All Dad
Starring Brave Rave

978-0-9973598-0-0

Editor: Janette Lonsdale, The Red Stairs
Illustrator: Aubrey Berkholtz
Design & Production: Eve Drueke and Peggy Nehmen

❋ Flower Press LLC
St. Louis, MO
BraveRaveBook.club
BraveRaveBook.com

Diary of a Diva's Daughter
with a
DO-IT-ALL DAD
Starring
Brave Rave

by Raquel Hunter

✾ Flower Press LLC

Search for a hidden letter or punctuation mark at the beginning of each chapter page.

At the end of the book, you'll be ready to spell out a secret phrase on these friendship bracelets.

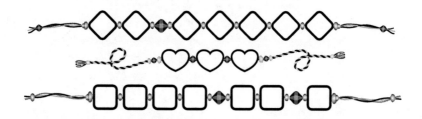

Answer on the last page - no cheating!

Property of

Raven Hunter

a.k.a.

Brave Rave

If found...
Seriously... Seriously...
DO NOT TOUCH!

Thank you

to all the people who have been part of
this experience — the good, the bad and the ALL.
I want to say a special thanks to my friends,
family, teachers and mentors who continued to
encourage me to be BRAVE through this journey.

May we all be
BRAVE & RAVE

The world is ours.

Give back.

TABLE OF CONTENTS

Chapter One

THE BEGINNING

I was told that in the beginning, my mom and dad were high school sweethearts. That just means they were all *lovey-dovey, kissy-kissy, mushy and gushy* in high school.

They were boyfriend and girlfriend. That's something I really don't want to think about. As much as I want to say **gross,** I really can't because I'm a product of their love. So it's not all the way gross.

Make no mistake. Boys are **super duper gross.** But my dad is not really gross. He is pretty awesome. My mom is too. Together, they are my parents, the **DO-IT-ALL DAD** and the **Diva Mom.**

There are lots of pictures of their life before me hanging on the walls all around our home. So I guess this is proof. I am their lovechild,

Raven.

←—me!

I was born at six in the morning.
I was perfect in every way —
six pounds, six ounces and
twenty inches long.

As soon as I came out, I opened my eyes
and looked at everyone, the doctor, the
nurse, and my dad. I blinked a couple of times and
then let out one or two strong cries.

Mom says the doctors gave me a *perfect* score on
my Apgar birth test. It scores you on how you look,
how loud you cry and if you blink as soon as you
come out of your mom. The test makes sure you are
healthy and *awesome*.

*Who knew you could be tested on being born? Really,
adults? A test?*

I guess this was just the preparation I needed for the
lifetime of forced testing I'd be thrown into with
school, sports, dance, and other stuff.

Deep sigh.

For as long as I can remember, these two have been pretty entertaining. They are my parents, the *DO-IT-ALL DAD* and **Diva Mom**.

I gave them these nicknames because they are true.

Evidence, you ask?

Wait for it.

...Wait for it.

Here are some pictures taken less than twelve hours after my birth. My **Diva Mom** had a bunch of glamorous gowns to change into, and she had a *make-up artist and hair stylist* on call for a family photo shoot as soon as I was born.

She even had my dad's wardrobe pre-selected and little bitty, custom-made, matching outfits for me, a one-day-old baby. She did all this so that we could blend into her glamorous idea of the *perfect family*.

And Dad was there, gleaming with pride, ready to support and encourage all her outlandish **Diva** ideas.

Seriously. Who does this?

No, but seriously. Who does this?

So began my journey as the daughter of a **DO-IT-ALL DAD** and **Diva Mom**.

Before you go on, dear reader, there is **one rule**.

You may laugh, chuckle and giggle at my story, but you cannot judge me. That is the only rule. I am just as shocked as you are by my life.

Every now and then I think about getting new parents.

Chapter Two

NEW PARENTS APPLY HERE

Applications for new parents are being accepted now:

From the desk of
RH

Name:

Do you eat meat?

Do you like ice cream and pizza?

Do you give allowances?

Can your child stay up after ten?

Do you think school is important?

How many pets can I have?

Do you like video games like Minecraft?

Do you yell?

Do I have to play in every sport known to man?

But then I get to thinking about how cool and fun my parents are most of the time. And about how uncool and mean other parents can be. Maybe most parents have to pass a parenting class like ***How to Be Mean*** or ***Be Tough on Your Kid*** or ***How to Punish Your Kid.***

As soon as I think I have it rough, I see another kid really, really going through it at the store or park or at school with their parents.

I suppose everyone has a moment or so when they are completely 🅰🅽🅽🅾🆈🅴🅳 by their family.

When it comes down to it, my ***DO-IT-ALL DAD*** and my **Diva Mom** are pretty *supreme beings.* And just like any other family, we have our good 🤍 and bad moments.

Keep reading to get a feel for my extraordinary *familia.* That is Spanish for the word family. I learned that in Spanish class along with the

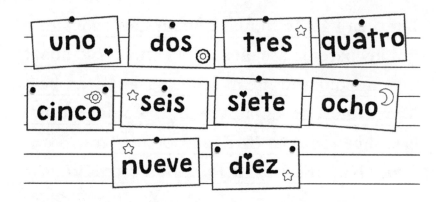

primary colors and how to count up to the number ten. Anyhow, let me give you a quick run-down on these two people.

I guess we should start with this lady, my mom, since she let me hang out in her belly for nine months. Yep. That's her, right there. The one who is glammed up to *superstar perfection* in every picture on the wall.

That is *Raquel Christine*. She is my **Diva Mom**.

Her father named her Raquel after a *beautiful* actress and model who was very popular in the olden days. I don't know how my grandma was okay with grandpa naming my mom after a strange woman, but she must have agreed to it. Seems awkward.

But whatever.

I think my mom even acts like a superstar **Diva**. Maybe it is because she is named after one? But I don't know. It's just a thought.

Mom has had an interesting and unusual list of jobs. I have memorized some of her jobs. Let's see. **Diva Mom** has been a:

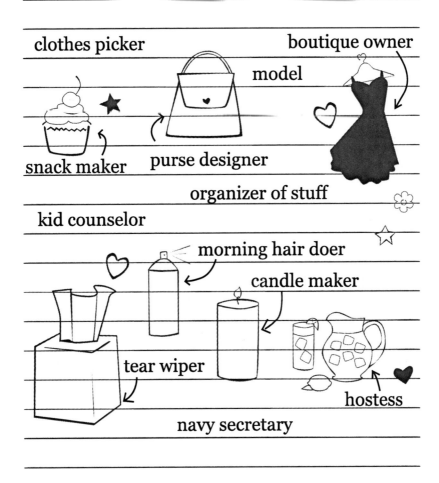

clothes picker

boutique owner

model

snack maker   purse designer

organizer of stuff

kid counselor

morning hair doer

candle maker

tear wiper

hostess

navy secretary

Oh yaaaah, and some other stuff that I don't know how to pronounce or spell. I am not totally sure what some of those jobs are or what she actually did but I just know she did them because she says so all the time. Some of them are things that she does for me. I think she adds **Diva**ism to all her jobs. That just means she makes them *pretty, exciting and cool.*

And now she is a **Diva** yoga instructor. She teaches people how to stretch, touch their toes and how to relax. She does it **Diva** style. That makes it funner and *prettier.*

Mom is always busy, BUSY, BUSY doing lots and lots of everything. But she is never too busy for me. I am her favorite person. I am *Raven.*

She says her biggest and most important job is being my mommy. I believe her. I am quite a BIG DEAL.

The only thing is, sometimes it doesn't seem like the rest of the world agrees. But my family and friends agree. I think that everyone else simply doesn't have a clue.

My life is pretty good. When Mom gets too much for me to handle, I turn to my *DO-IT-ALL DAD*. He is very special to me. ♡

My dad is a professional hair cutter. Well, a barber. He has been cutting hair since he was twelve or something. He practiced on his friends' hair until he got better and better. He says he slaughtered some haircuts in his younger days.

I feel sorry for his friends.

Eventually my dad became a professional barber. Now he has his own barbershop. The other barbers in the shop jokingly call my dad the BARBER-BOSS. That nickname makes me feel so proud. I can tell he likes it too.

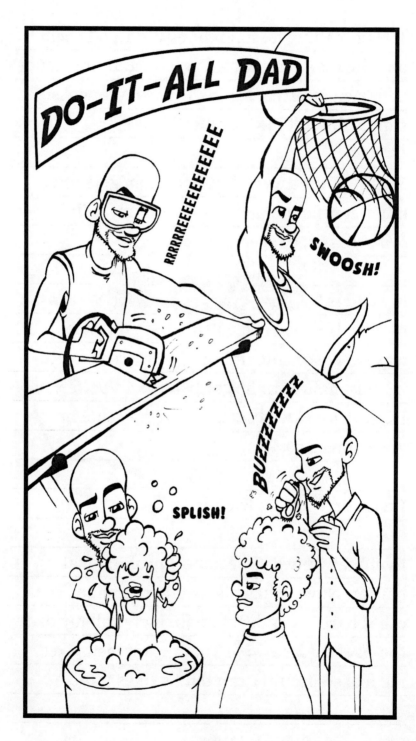

When Dad is not at the barbershop he is around the house building and fixing stuff. He knows how to do everything in **DUDE STYLE**. Well, almost everything.

My **DO-IT-ALL DAD** fixes cars, grills yummy food and runs super fast because he is an athlete. And to top it off, he can build **COOL STUFF** like my tree house.

Except my tree house is not in a tree at all because my mom says,

"It's not safe to be up that high."

I don't agree and neither does dad.

Chapter Three

MY PLAY HOUSE

When Dad and I play together we have so much fun. We go WILD. We play hide-and-go-seek in the dark and play sharks in the pool. In the yard we play ball and SWORD FIGHT.

He rarely sets limitations and restrictions on our play — unlike someone I know. That would be Mom.

She is always insisting, "I do not have time in my day to take either of you to the hospital."

I think she worries too much.

For now the tree house is on the ground. Why? Because Mom says so. That's all there is to it.

So I actually have a play house, not a tree house.

My play house is still the best, even if it is on the ground. Having a little place that is all my own, that is away from the house, is cool.

Well, it is almost all my own. My parents seem to have a welcome pass that NEVER EXPIRES.

But I understand. It really is just such a *perfect* space. It's just right for me and my world of FUN!

Dad let me help design it. He asked me, "What do you really want in your play house?"

"A comfy place to draw and lie down with my pets and dolls," I said.

And he built it *just right*. He added a built-in table and bench and he even put in a little kitchen with cabinets in the corner. It's really neat. It definitely serves its purpose for preparation and cleanup after my *tea parties* with my pets and stuffed animals.

I call them *tea parties* but I am not a fan of tea. I only drink it when I'm not feeling well, and I don't even do that until it's almost too late for it to make me feel better. So I fill my teapot and teacups with apple and grape juice. Kool-Aid or soda would be nice, but Mom won't allow that.

My favorite tea party guests, without a doubt, are my spunky guinea pig GIZMO, my very protective dog CAESAR and my stuffed animals. Gizmo and Caesar both get along well with each other. And if I give them their favorite snacks, they behave, stay still and munch. They will even allow me to *dress them up in clothes*. It's fun. They love the play house. We all do.

But of course Mom helped to make it what it is too. She is the *grand decorator* of all things — in her mind anyway. She bought a little cozy couch that fits just right, a bunch of pillows and some cool pictures to hang on the walls.

She called what she was doing the *icing on the cake*. That just means it's even more sweet than regular.

She even took before and after pictures of my little play house to showcase her *supreme decorating* and Dad's building skills.

She shows the pictures to everyone. I think she is BRAGGING when she does this, but I would never say that to her.

They always say bragging is **SO wrong**.

Without those pictures, no one would know what my place even looks like. I never invite folks over to my little play house because I really don't have any friends. People are nice to play with at school, but other than that, I am not so sure about them being in my personal space.

Privacy Please

I don't know why I don't have any friends I like enough to hang out with. I JUST DON'T. I have tried. But I'm not worried because Mom and Dad hang out with me ALL THE TIME, even when I don't necessarily want them to.

My space is *perfect* the way it is.

Please just leave **my** space alone.

Raven's House
♥ welcome!

Remember, this is my PRIVATE play house.

Chapter Four
CHESS IS LIFE

Can you imagine what life is like with this **Diva** and *DO-IT-ALL*? I could not make this stuff up. They are this way without even trying.

I am not a **Diva** or a *DO-IT-ALL*. Nor do I want to be. If I become a **Diva** or *DO-IT-ALL* it will be because my parents made me that way.

Some of the things they expect from me are completely and utterly EXTREME.

Mom has me at *ballet* twice on Saturdays. I have piano and swim class after school during the week and she is talking about adding ice skating to the list.

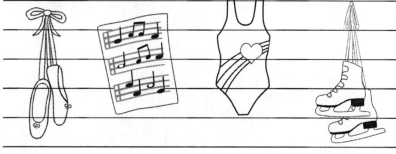

It's a lot for a kid, right?

Chess is boring.

One more time.

CHESS.

IS.

BORING.

I will never, ever, ever tell Dad that his favorite board game is tragically boring. I don't want to disappoint him or hurt his feelings. I can save that sort of let-down for something that is a lot more meaningful to me.

So I will continue to hang in there, suffer through the boredom and smile, and play chess with him.

It is not such a huge deal because it's just one more thing I can add to my "I know how to do" list.

I know how to do a lot of things *pretty well*. Lots of things come pretty easily to me: *reading, math, and drawing*, just to name a few. All I have to do is pay attention and give my one hundred percent and try and keep trying, because *practice makes perfect* — or close to perfect.

But there are times when I just don't wanna do anything.

NOT A THING! No.

I just want to sit in my room and draw, play video games or *play with my animals*. Or just hang out in my play house alone.

These adults have all these BIG PLANS that involve me doing EVERYTHING.

I wouldn't wish these shenanigans on the meanest girl.

Please, folks, can I get some time to myself? How do I earn some  downtime?

All the while other kids are doing whatever, and I mean whatever, they want. What gives?

I will tell you what gives — other kids have a regular mom and dad. I have a **DO-IT-ALL DAD** and a **Diva Mom**.

My mom always comes up with ideas for me to stay ACTIVE.

What does active even mean?

I play with my animals. I play chess with Dad. I play video games like Minecraft. I draw.

I am reading a book, like, all the time. I write in my diary. I even ride my bike.

I AM ACTIVE.

Seriously! That is what she is like.

She makes sure that she receives catalogs from every recreation center in and near our town just to see what classes she can stick me in next. She wants to overload my life against my will.

You would think that she would be exhausted driving me to all these places. But apparently it gives her great joy.

She makes me do all these things and Dad doesn't say a word in my defense. Instead, he is smiling and rooting me on to do my best, to focus and to try hard. I wonder why he doesn't save me from the 𝔇𝔦𝔳𝔞'𝔰 wrath. I think they are both on team *Exhaust the Child*. Maybe it is because he is such a **DO-IT-ALL** he thinks this is normal too?
Well, it is not normal!

When she was my age she did hardly any activities because grandma and grandpa could not afford them. And she turned out *just fine.*

I hardly complain at all because there are great *perks* to doing what my parents want. When I do what they ask and try hard, I get to spend the day at the pet store or at an *old-time candy shop* or get left alone to do my own thing for a little bit.

So I smile. I try my best. Then I wait for my reward. It's a formula that typically works.

I say yes = Parents say yes.

Chapter Five

PRACTICE MAKES PERFECT

Ballet, ice skating, soccer, golf, swimming and horseback riding lessons all in one school year. Did I mention that I am just seven years old?

The **messed - up** part is that you don't just practice. You have to PERFORM.

At some point you are expected to showcase the skills you've learned. You have to take part in a

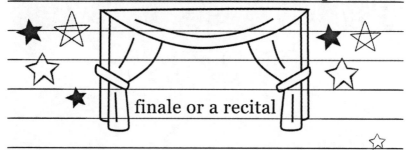

finale or a recital

or a big game in front of a bunch of people that you don't even know.

I really didn't sign up for this, but I just never quite know how to say no to my parents. When the moment arrives for me to disagree, I cannot say a solid NO.

If I am not buzzed to do what they want me to
do, they double-team me. Mom will offer me
something she knows I really want. Or Dad will
persuade me by giving me a pep talk about
being the best me I can be and trying new
things. They have some type of mind- and
mood- changing powers ...

NOT FAIR — it's two against one!

And now they even have my grandma Val on their side. She always took my side no matter what. At least that was the way it went in my head. But I have noticed that she invites me over for Sunday lunch and has this lovely spread of food and treats.

She says all the right things and closes with...

Honey we are from the Show Me State, so show the world what you can do.

At school I learned that every state has a little logo or slogan. Missouri is the Show Me State. Thanks a lot, Missouri, for giving Grandma Val the ammunition to say I need to show

I can't catch a break.

Like with this soccer thing. I always enjoy kicking a ball in the grass when the sun is shining and it's not too hot. Who doesn't?

But Mom had this clever idea.

She wanted me to play soccer at school because some of the parents started a kids team.

Mom thought it would be good for me to try a team sport. She claimed it would teach me the value of being a part of a team. Sure, I will try something new, especially if the reward is right.

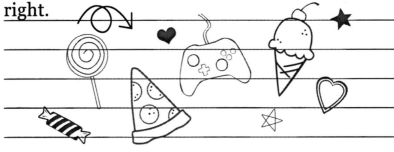

Soccer began as an okay game. During soccer practice our team would just play around with the ball, kicking it and trying to get it into the goal. All my teammates are friends from school.

There are eight boys and three girls on my team. Two of the kids are chunky, and one kid wears glasses that keep falling off.

We know how to have fun playing soccer.

We have three coaches — one mom and two dads. Their kids are on the team. All the parents and coaches have made a *BIG DEAL* about all the kids wearing the same-color shirt so that we will feel and look like a team when we eventually play against another team.

Same-color shirts. That works, I guess.

Today we are playing our first game against another team. I wonder how long this will take? The reward has been established already — pet store visit. Well, Mom is calling me down now. I will tell you all about our win later!

I am really looking forward to the *pet store* visit so I can play with the hamsters and guinea pigs. They let you hold and pet the animals if you want.

Chapter Six
THE
SOCCER GAME

I'm BACK.

Guess what?

There were so many people.

Who were they? And why did they want to watch us play? We are just learners. We are not even good ball-kickers.

Everyone was hanging out on the field. Grown ups were grilling food and they had their lawn chairs out. Some little kids were playing tag.

The only people I knew even a tiny bit were my own teammates. Even with all the strangers it looked like a party. *I love parties*.

The only thing I wanted was for Mom to save me a hot dog and a juice. No worries there, because I knew she would do that even without me asking.

A good athlete keeps a healthy appetite — that's what my dad says while eating mountains of food.

I took my time and scanned the field. The sun was beaming. There was a soft, *warm breeze.*

I figured the good weather was a sign that things would be *awesome.*

It was a *perfect day.*

It felt so *magical.*

Our team was ready.

The assistant coach made us stretch. That felt good.

But I could see the other team getting ready. They weren't doing stupid stretches. They were practicing passing the ball to one another.

I got lost in my stretch as I watched them.

Wow. We never do anything like that.

They are not beginners. Who are these guys?

Why are we playing in the big league?

Uh-oh. We have BIG KIDS.

At least two of my teammates are playing
soccer because they are fat and they need to
lose weight because their doctors said so.
We have three girls, including me. Us girls are
fast, but were are not good at kicking the ball
yet. More practice would be needed. Wonder
if the kids on that team are mean? I can't
really tell.

By the looks of it, that team was REALLY
SERIOUS. Maybe that's why they didn't have
girls? #SeriousBusinessHere #NoGirlsAllowed

Hmm . . . they were wearing
matching team uniforms —
tall socks with cushion
kneepads. Their team shirts had
names on the backs just like in
the big leagues. They even had soccer shoes
on. Real soccer shoes — like the professionals.
They all looked really serious about this game.
Did anyone else see what I could see?

None of my other teammates or coaches looked concerned at all. So I rejected any **negative thoughts** that came into my head and replaced them with only thoughts of winning.

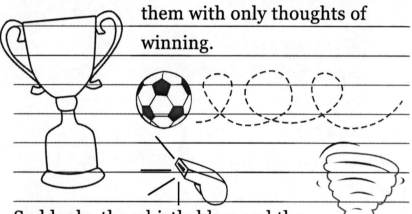

Suddenly, the whistle blew and the game began. Both teams ran to get the ball. I just knew someone was going to get hurt because everyone was running this way and that trying to get the ball.

There were way too many people going after this one ball — super unsafe. I couldn't imagine that my mom wanted me to continue to run towards danger just to get a ball. It was bad enough that all the kids on the other team were so much bigger than me.

I still was confident that we could win this game because we always try hard, we work together and we are good kids.

We were hoping that someone from our team would kick the ball into the net. Everyone began to tussle for the ball. It was getting rough. Everyone was moving so fast, arms flying and legs kicking.

But please explain why would I run towards something these big kids wanted so bad? Was this a joke? I turned to look for my mom on the sidelines — should I be doing this?

Maybe she did want me to run towards the ball? But she always told me never to follow people off a cliff into danger, no matter who they are. She told me to march to the beat of my own drum and lead.

Still, I needed to get a little confirmation on what to do. **Diva Mom** was way too far away and she wasn't watching the game at that exact moment. She had set up her video camera not far from her, but she was at the grill turning meat with another player's mom.

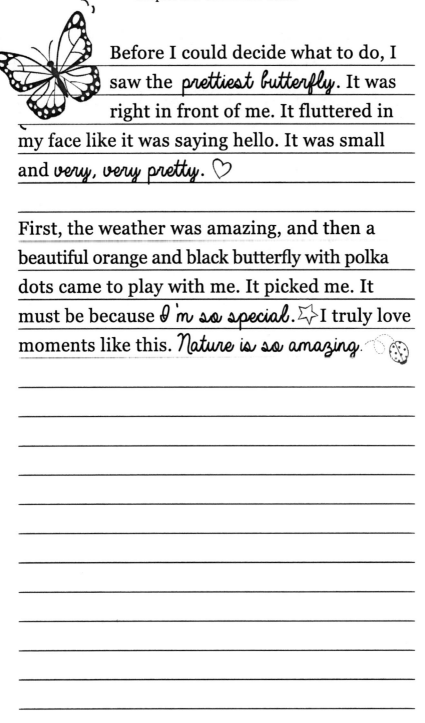

Before I could decide what to do, I saw the *prettiest butterfly*. It was right in front of me. It fluttered in my face like it was saying hello. It was small and *very, very pretty.* ♡

First, the weather was amazing, and then a beautiful orange and black butterfly with polka dots came to play with me. It picked me. It must be because *I'm so special.* ✰ I truly love moments like this. *Nature is so amazing.*

Right in the face.

Someone from the other team had given the ball the hardest-ultimate-POWER KICK. The ball flew straight to my face like a magnet.

STATUS: Bloody, busted lip and tears.
FEELING: Embarrassed.

I was taken to my mom on the sideline. Mom dried my tears and tried to stop the bleeding with a cloth from the portable first aid kit.

She gave me a fruit drink. The drink actually eased the pain. I guess you can't feel pain and eat and enjoy something at the same time. Mom said, *"There, there, you'll be okay."*

She said I must give such a physical game my full attention. No one looked disappointed or mad at me. The whistle blew and the game started again. Without me! *What a relief.*

My team continued to play.

Was I the weak link because I'm so small?
Was the butterfly okay?
Could the butterfly have been part of the other team's plan?
Did it distract me on purpose?
Will I see the butterfly again?

Mom told me that it was okay, but I must give such a physical game my full attention. No one looked disappointed or mad at me. My team continued to play.

Am I a weak link because I'm so small? Is the butterfly okay? If I'm as special as Mom and Dad say, why did this happen to me?

My mind was going everywhere.

If I am so special, like Mom and Dad say I am, why did this happen to me?

Just when I was starting to wrestle with this idea and while my mom and I were talking and hugging, two old ladies came up to me.

I glanced at Mom and she was nodding her head as if she was saying yes in her head.

HUH?
SHE AGREES WITH THEM!

The old ladies reached in for a hug and patted me on my back.

Mom said, "Beloved, be brave. It will be okay. You just have to apply yourself and watch the ball."

She calls me *"Beloved,"* when she is about to cry.

I really didn't want to disappoint my mom or the pretty old ladies. They said that if I didn't go back out there I would be a **quitter**.

If I quit every time I get hurt, then I will miss out on getting the things I want really bad.

"In life you may **fall, get scratched, bruised and hurt**, but if your habit is to dust yourself off and get back up and out there, you can succeed," the old ladies said.

Mom added, "My little Brave Rave, you can do it!"

I slumped. I slowly walked to join my team and got back into the game.

Behind me I could hear the old ladies chanting.

"GO BRAVE RAVE."

"GO BRAVE RAVE."

They must have heard my mom call me that. Brave Rave is my superhero name. Everyone should have a superhero name.

That name was easy to pick. It is the only name that rhymes with my nickname, Rave.

I AM BRAVE RAVE.

I did not try as hard this time. I didn't want to get hurt again. No more of my blood would spill today.

But I did go back out on the field and finish the game. Just like everyone told me to. Finishing the game felt good. I was really brave.

Go Brave Rave!
Go Brave Rave!
Go Brave Rave!

I could feel a smile on my face. But it wasn't an ordinary smile. It was my let's-get-through-this-and-get-this-over-with smile.

Once I made it to the field the crowd clapped. I got in the game. I hung in there until the end.

We lost the game by fourteen goals.

A busted lip and tears, all to be losers.

I looked for the butterfly but I didn't see her again.

I am so happy the game is over. Soccer is just not my thing.

On the drive home Mom stopped for ice cream because, after everything that happened, I really didn't want to go to the pet store. I just wanted to get home.

She told me over and over and over, again and again, "The lesson is to be attentive and focused and not allow yourself to get distracted, Raven."

That's easy for her to say. She didn't see that pretty butterfly.

All I know is that I don't like playing soccer.

You can scratch that off the list.

Watching is okay, but playing — I don't think so.

To make matters worse — it is all on video. This will haunt me forever. They'll probably show it at my next birthday party or a family gathering.

I hope Mom is real happy now. I am active and I got hurt. I hope this is a lesson for her and that from now on she'll let me play my way. I hope it gets me out of soccer?

But wait, there is MORE.

I remember it all.

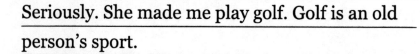

Ice skating.
Swim/dive lessons.
The cooking classes.
Even golf lessons.

Seriously. She made me play golf. Golf is an old person's sport.

Even the horse riding lessons.

70

Chapter Seven
HORSES ARE MAGICAL

Did I tell you about the time when Mom signed me up for horseback riding lessons?

She missed the registration date for the kids' group classes that I wanted to take with Zora. She is my buddy from school.

Before I knew what was going on, Mom signed me up for horseback riding lessons she found on her own. She said I wouldn't be taking the lesson with Zora. That didn't really matter to me. Horses are magical and cool. I just love them.

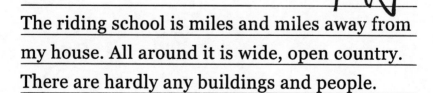

Our drive was very, very long. Mom said this would be an every-Saturday journey if the first lesson went well.

The riding school is miles and miles away from my house. All around it is wide, open country. There are hardly any buildings and people.

When we got there, Mom pulled slowly into the

parking lot. The driveway wasn't blacktop like in the city; instead, there were lots and lots of little pebbles.

We sat in the car while Mom got organized — keys, checkbook, lipstick and tea tumbler. Oh yeah, and ABOUT THIS TEA TUMBLER...

Diva Mom's tea tumbler

HANDS OFF!

Handle with Care!

Tasty Treats Only

For Diva Mom Only

She takes it everywhere she goes!

And the speech began.

"Pay attention."

"Don't get distracted."

"Speak up if you're uncomfortable or have a question."

We went into the office to speak to Mrs. Kathy. She is the horseback riding teacher. She is also the owner.

The office has a balcony with a window that looks over the main corral. I looked down and I could see a rider on her horse and her teacher.

They were doing jumps, and the horse marched in circles over and over again.

While I was watching all the horse action, a small, old dog and a fat cat nuzzled my legs until I gave them a rub. Maybe it was their job to greet people? I just cuddled these pets right back. I love pets so much.

All my attention was on the pets and not on the girl and horse practicing below.

I had a hunch I would like it here.

Mom wrote a check to the lady while keeping an eye on me with the cat and dog.

For a second, my hand stopped petting the animals.
Wait. What? Kill who? Is she talking about me?

I caught my mom's eye. Who would come out
of this panic-stare first? It's usually Mom. But
this time it was me.

Mom looked like she was about to grab me and
run. I've never seen her look that way before.
She asked me, "Do you still want to try this?"
I swallowed and took a breath. "Yes, let's try it."
Mom's face looked unusually scared. I think
she secretly wanted me to beg to go home.

I mean this is what I have been waiting for — I wanted to ride a horse. I figured if the cat and dog were so friendly, the horse would be too, and I would be okay.

We walked down to the stable, and the teacher gave me a horse. She told me to lead the horse from his stall to the grooming station for a pre-ride groom.

Yippee! I've got a horse. His name is Champion.

Mrs. Ross explained that horses love to be groomed and that grooming is a big part of riding. The rider must groom her animal before and after every ride to bond with the horse. It is the horse's reward.

No problem, I brush hair all the time, thanks to my massive Culture Chic Doll collection and my pets. My dog and my guinea pig love getting brushed. This will be easy.

The teacher showed me how to groom. I watched her every move. I paid very close attention. Finally, it was my turn.

I was good at this. I could do this all by myself. I wasn't scared at all. I looked at Mom to make sure she was watching how good I was

at grooming. But instead of looking proud, she was clenching her bag and her tea tumbler.

Without a doubt, Mom was tense. She was sipping her drink every couple of seconds. She looked like she was doing secret breathing exercises to keep from freaking all the way out.

I know about the breathing exercises because she's tried to teach them to me to help me combat my nervousness — it is called *meditation.*

Deep, slow, inhale and exhale.

Mom didn't seem relaxed. She stood sipping from her tea tumbler.
She sipped every few seconds.
Poor Mom. Relax. Look at me.

It was great, because it gave me the opportunity to teach Mom to be **brave** today.

Horses are so big and beautiful.

Champion has a red coat and long, black mane. I wanted to braid it so badly.

This is the first time I have been up close, one-on-one, with a horse. I hope he likes me.

79

He is so big; the top of my head barely reaches the bottom of his mouth. I led Champion from his stall to a grooming station so I could brush him before my ride. ♡

I brushed him just like Mrs. Kathy showed me.

While I brushed him, I was daydreaming about him running through fields when he started to step lightly, over and over, in the same spot. Champion was slowly marching in place. He was also making noises.

Was I doing something wrong? I paused brushing, "Is this normal?" I asked.

"It's a sign he likes you," said Mrs. Kathy.

BEEP. BEEP. BEEP. Mom's calendar alert went off to notify her this activity was over.

I watched Mom turning off the phone alert. She seemed almost back to normal. I know she was relieved that this was over.

We took Champion back to his stall.

A full lesson of grooming and no ride, huh? Well, I'll be back next week to ride him.

We said goodbye to Champion and
my teacher. I gave him one last
pat on his side and we scurried to the car.

I was just getting comfortable in the back seat
when Mom said firmly, "You will not be going
back there."

So a riding lesson without an actual ride and she said we aren't returning.

DEEP SIGH!

Wait, I never got a chance to say goodbye to the friendly dog and the fat cat.

On the drive home, I asked no questions. Mom was in her rant mode, so I made no attempt to disagree with her decision. I knew what would happen if I interrupted. She would get frustrated with me. So I remained quiet and gazed out the window.

I just wanted to get home to my own pets. I love my pet family: my guinea pig Gizmo and my dog Caesar.

Chapter Eight
THE PET GALLERY

One thing that is great about my parents is they let me keep animals. I have been allowed to have so many different pets. It's because I am an only child.

I love my animals. They are precious, special and very unique.

I used to want a little sister or brother really, really bad. Every day I'd ask Mom — at the store, at the doctor's office, at the park — "Can you have a baby, please?"

She didn't understand how much fun it would be to have another ME. Her reply was always the same — a giggle and "I don't think so sweetie," followed with, "you will understand when you get older."

She told me it was really painful and hard to have a baby. I don't get it. It doesn't look so tough to me.

But I think she must have really felt guilty because she started to take me to the pet store every time I asked for a sister or brother. It was brilliant. I'd come home with a pet or a pet book so I could learn about my next pet.

Eventually I stopped asking Mom about having another ME. I was sort of busy and preoccupied with all my pets. I had to feed them and take care of them.

It is too late now to have a sister or brother my age – they'd be too small to be a real playmate and partner in crime. It wouldn't be much fun helping to take care of a baby.

Thanks, Mom, for feeling guilty about not wanting more children. I have had so many cool pets.

I had two African scorpions. Those are the ones that are not poisonous but they are the largest of their species. They were really cool to watch. I never held them. Scorpions just aren't the cuddly type.

My fire-bellied toads were bright and pretty. They ate nothing but crickets.

Then I had a fish, a turtle and after that I got hamsters.

I've had my big dog for years and years, and now I also have a guinea pig.

My dog's name is Caesar the American Bulldog. My guinea pig's name is Gizmo. They both have the same color fur. They are mostly white with light brown patches and smaller black patches.

Caesar is a super big, tough guard dog. He is more of a  house dog. He hates going outside for more than a few minutes unless he is going for a walk or with his human family. He is a very, very big and pretty dog.

I have loved him since we first got him when I was three. He is very protective. He won't let anyone get close to us unless he knows them.

When we take Caesar for a walk people honk their horns at us.

They stop in traffic and ask questions about him.

"How much does your dog weigh?"

"What type of dog is that?"

"Is your dog a girl or boy?"

The questions people ask always end with compliments about Caesar's good looks. That makes my dad so proud. They say Caesar is a very handsome dog.

Once when we were walking Caesar, a group of teenage girls drove past us, honking and hanging out of the car windows shouting:

"That dog is hot!" And then they all howled.

What does that mean? A dog — hot.

And why were they howling?

Teenage girls are weird.

My dog is cute maybe, handsome certainly, but I don't think it is good for him to feel too hot. Just strangeness.

People even stop us to ask if their girl dog can be Caesar's wife! They want him to make puppies with their dog.

So gross.

Caesar would be a father and a husband?

That is so funny to imagine.

Dad always says a firm, "No, thank you," to the breeding and having puppies. Mom says that there isn't a girl dog pretty enough for our Caesar to marry.

See what I mean? Everyone treats Caesar like he is a human.

He is part of my family, and he is my brother.

Since forever, when I wake up in the morning and before doing anything else, I go give Caesar hugs and cuddles. Even before I give Mom and Dad morning kisses and hugs.

He takes baths and gets his nails trimmed. Dad brushes his teeth once a week. He gets treats. We don't even leave him outside for long.

As soon as he barks, he is saying, "Let me back in," and someone lets him back inside.

He cries if we don't come to the door to let him in.

If we leave him home alone he puts on a whole ATTITUDE when we get back. He tries to ignore us by laying with his back to us and HUFFS AND PUFFS when we start talking. That's the way humans act too.

When I was younger, I would tell people he was my brother. I thought that because my parents always referred to Caesar as their son. I didn't know any better.

Once, my teacher asked our class to share stuff about our families. When the teacher asked me whether I had a sister or brother, my honest response was, "Yes, I have a younger brother named Caesar."

At a parent-teacher meeting, my teacher asked about my brother's age. My mom laughed and then explained my sibling confusion. For some reason, these two adults thought my confusion was hilarious and laughed about it way too hard and WAY TOO LONG. ⏱ Mom went on to share this story with anyone who would listen. I was so embarrassed.

Mom and Dad explained it to me like this: Caesar is a big part of our family. He is my animal brother and their animal son. He is not my human brother or their human son.

So now I don't tell people that I have a brother. This limits the confusion. But I still love him so much. ♡ ♥ ♡ ♡

It would have really been nice if they had clarified all this in the beginning. It would have saved me so much embarrassment.

I would like to bring Caesar to school for a show-and-tell class. But he is so protective he would probably bite all my school friends if they got too close to me. See, he is like a brother.

I brought Gizmo, my guinea pig, to school instead. I hope Caesar doesn't get jealous.

Gizmo is a G.W.A. (Guinea pig With an Attitude). I knew this when I picked him out at the pet store — he was the only one with a mohawk.

Yes, a MOHAWK.

A guinea pig with a mohawk that sticks up. So rad.

He is lovable but doesn't have much patience. When he sees fresh lettuce and carrots he goes insane and squeaks loudly. If you take too long bringing food to his mouth he will yank it out of your grip with his teeth.

Attitude for sure.

My class enjoyed seeing him because he has so much personality. Plus, a guinea pig with a mohawk is a sight to be seen.

All the kids took turns holding and petting him. For a day Gizmo was a superstar and my classmates were the super fans.

He sucked the attention up too. I enjoyed seeing my school buddies happy playing with my guinea pig.

I didn't mind sharing him.

He makes me happy.

Chapter Nine

A NEW SCHOOL

I love, love, love ♡ my school, but it doesn't teach past the first grade, so this is my very last summer here. I am seven years old and I am going into second grade.

When I started first grade I thought it was really cool to be in a grade with a whole number. And second grade is an even higher number.

I am moving in the right direction and maturing. That's what Mom says. Sounds scary, but I think it means I am ready for second grade.

I should probably ask someone. Those snacks throughout the day really can hit the spot when my tummy is growling. And the naps come just

before everyone gets grumpy and stops sharing toys and books with each other.

Aahh, naps!

I guess I could ask
Mom about the nap
and snack thing.

Mom was so busy trying to pick my new school.
It made us all sort of nervous. At least I was.

There will be a new building, new teachers,
new kids and new rules — sheesh. That is a lot
of new for a girl to handle.

Before the school was picked,
Mom sat in and observed
Miss Laura's second
grade class for several hours
throughout the week. She saw
how the teacher taught and
dealt with the kids. Miss Laura was happy and
upbeat. She made learning exciting.

Mom says Miss Laura gets two thumbs up.

Mom loves her teaching style.

Mom was so excited. I will be going to the exact same school she went to when she was my age.

I'm so excited! You'll be going to the same school I went to when I was your age!

She keeps telling Dad and me that she had some wonderful times at that school with her favorite teachers, some really great friends and lots of fun playground games. She made me very interested to see what this school was really about.

Mom went to the school over twenty years ago. I wonder if much has changed?

I bet it has, because Mom says when she was little cell phones didn't even exist. Now that is a long time ago.

She says there was no Internet and everyone played outside and read books written on paper.

Can you imagine? The first time she mentioned there was no Internet, video games and cell phones when she was a child, I thought she was joking.

When I am with my parents and I get bored I ask to see their cell phones so I can play video games. I just wonder what kids did back then when they

were stuck with their parents at the doctors'
offices or on a long drive.

Mom insists that those were the good old days.
She also insists her school was awesome.

My mom is pretty *excellent,* so the school
must be all right.

She calls the new school "public." Public means
that any kid can go there for free as long as you
live close by. My old school was a private school.
The parents had to pay for kids to go to it.

Because our parents had to pay for us to go
there, we all followed the rules. The last thing
we wanted was for the teacher or the head of
the school to call home.

I watch adults and I can see they are very serious about their money. They hate spending it but love having it. A smart kid knows not to come between an adult and too much of their money.

Private or public, school is just school, right?

I am a little sad that I will no longer see my friends and teachers. I have been with them since I was four years old. But it is time for us to leave, so I am bracing myself for the change. Now what?

I wonder if the kids at my new school will be smart and friendly? Will they be into arts and crafts?

It's not a private school like your school now. It's public, which means anyone can attend.

I wonder if the kids at my new school are smart and friendly.

Or into sports? Or like animals and insects? Will they like me?

The night before I started my new school, my Auntie Ashley, my mom's younger sister, came by with a gift. I absolutely love when she visits because she brings me one-of-a-kind presents. This time my auntie came into my room with a big bag of new outfits so I could wear something fabulous on my first day.

I was so excited. I emptied the bag out onto my bed. I immediately picked the skater skirt and long-sleeved shirt. I would wear them with my favorite boots.

To top it off she handed me some amazing pencils that she'd painted with swirls and polka dots.

Some of the pencils even had *glitter* on them. I loved them. They were just what I needed.

Suddenly I did not feel so nervous. I was ready. My outfit was picked. Thank you, Auntie Ashley.

When I arrived at school it was LOUD. Everything made noise. Bells, intercom announcements, kids shouting in the hall, kids on buses, even some of the teachers were loud.

I wondered how I would get through the day. I made my way to Room 12, my classroom. I sat down at my desk; it had my name on it.

The teacher closed the door and began to talk to us. That is when I realized how I would get through that day and every other day. She would help me.

Her room had a great calm to it. She even had pets — a rabbit and a hamster — in her class.

I wondered if kids were allowed to sit on that big beanbag near the window. This was beyond my expectations. Her voice was so warm and cozy. Her smile was friendly.

I enjoyed listening to her talk and wondered what she would say next.

It was even better once I realized that we would get snacks throughout the day. Any snack is better than no snack. We get pretzels, cheese crackers and peanut butter crackers.

Nap time was not a part of the deal anymore. But that was all right with me as long as the snacks continued to flow.

I'm going to nail second grade.

I don't think that I will ever get used to the loud bells.

piece of cake Second grade is so easy. I am sure that I'll get all the gold stars. I enjoy doing my worksheets because I understand most of the work.

Plus, who could resist a reason to use my awesome pencils?

They make doing my work so lovely this year. My aunt, who is an artist, made them. Each pencil is painted with sparkles and swirls in pink, blue and yellow. My favorite colors. My pencils are so beautiful. *Princess perfect*. They guarantee I will get top marks.

. . . because I know I will have a gold star clipped onto my paper. I can put it next to my name on the success chart.

At this school we get gold stars for being quiet and following directions. Stars are not just for graded work.

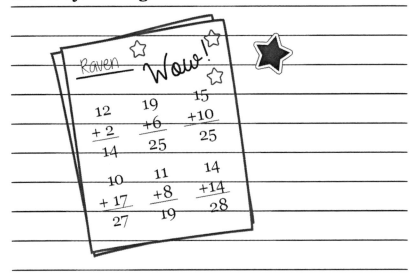

Chapter Ten

RING RING RECESS

"It's lunch time, young people. Stop what you are working on and put everything in your desk," said Miss Laura.

I put all my belongings away just as she asked and I quietly sat with my hands folded on top of my desk. All I had to do was top it off with a soft smile and hopeful eyes.

Mom tells me that my hopeful eyes and smile will get me anything I want in the world. I have been trying this out and it works every time. Well, most of the time.

All I could think about was going outside for recess. I wasn't really hungry today, but I did really want to go outside to play.

So I was going to wolf down my lunch, go outside and be the first kid at the jump ropes.

The jump ropes with the yellow handles were newer and I only saw two of them.

And yup, I was going for a yellow-handle rope. So watch out, everyone.

Ms. Laura stood watching the class as she decided who deserved to be line leader.

"Come on. Come on, come on," I shouted in my head. *"Pick me!"*

Ms. Laura paused and called my name. *"Raven!"*

I popped out of my seat, pushed my chair in and made it over to the door at the same time as Delvin.

He is *that* kid. The one no one wants to be friends with because he is just a big meanie. You don't want to be on the wrong side of his wrath. He makes the teachers frustrated and kids cry.

I just wonder if even his parents like him?

Every so often Miss Laura shows her frustration with him. I can hear her sigh when he is acting out. It's like she takes a deep breath and gathers herself to deal with him.

I bet she wishes he wasn't in her class. I know that I do.

Delvin stood in first place.

(UM, WHAT?)

He stayed at the front of the line even though he knew Miss Laura called me first. I was the line leader today.

As much as I wanted to steer clear of Delvin I had to stand up to him.

So I said, "I am line leader, excuse me," and I got in front of him.

Phew, that went well. He did not flip out or go crazy.

Miss Laura continued to call the rest of the students to get in the line — I was the line leader. 1st!

"You can't always be a line leader, it's my turn," Delvin hissed.

I ignored him because I knew that he was trying to get me to talk so Miss Laura would catch me and remove me from being line leader.

I am smarter than that. Ha ha, I have watched Delvin do this to other kids when he is second in line. He is a clever cookie. But I am smarter.

I glanced down at my shoes and noticed they were untied. I hurried to tie my shoes before the line needed to get moving. Plus, I didn't want Delvin to hop back in front of me because I was tying my shoes. He was not getting in front of me.

Shoe-Tie Rhyme

Bunny ears, bunny ears, playing by a tree.
Criss-crossed the tree, trying to catch me.
Bunny ears, bunny ears, jumped into the hole,
popped out the other side
beautiful and bold.

All done. "Wait. Does that look right?" I said
quietly in my head.

As I got up, I suddenly felt a poke from behind.
I already knew it was Delvin. I turned around.
Out of the corner of my eye I saw sparkly swirls
on something. It looked like a pencil. It was. It
was my pencil.

MY PENCIL!

I could hear Delvin whisper, "I hate you, goodie two-shoes."

I raised my hand in a panic. I mean, that is my pencil. When did he take it?

"Yes, Raven," said Miss Laura.

"Delvin stole my pencil and just said to me he hates me," I said.

Telling was all I knew how to do. Things were a bit out of control. This guy took my pencil and said mean things to me. What gives? My old school was full of fun friends. I have never met anyone like Delvin. What should I do?

I usually don't like to see kids get into trouble but this guy deserves some sort of punishment. I wonder if Miss Laura will call his parents or if he will have to have lunch with the principal.

Miss Laura sighed and firmly said, "Delvin, come with me right now."

She had me lead the class to the lunchroom. And I knew the way there all by myself. I was feeling PROUD to be the leader, but I was a little anxious about what just happened with Delvin. He would not forget this easily.

I was just dipping into my cherry
Jell-O cup when Delvin appeared.
Seeing him put me off my Jell-O.

He was back, just like that, and he was looking for a
place to sit. He sat right across from me.

He was giving me the death stare as I ate my Jell-O.
I felt a kick under the table. I knew he did it.

126

Well I am not buying it. This has nothing to do with like. When you like a person you show her by being just that — NICE to them, not MEAN.

Delvin is a supreme hater.

"Delvin. Stop kicking me!" I said with irritation.

He didn't even attempt to respond. Instead he quickly leaned over and whispered to the person on his left and then to the kid on the right.

All I could hear him say was, "Pass it on." I began to hear "eeewhhhhh" from the other kids around me as they told the secret to the next person. It was as if everyone was playing the game of telephone.

Eventually, the message reached me. The kid next to me leaned over and chuckled, "Delvin says Raven kissed him in the mouth and she let him touch her butt."

My eyes popped, my mouth dropped open, my eyes started to sting and fill with tears. It was official. I lost my appetite.

IRKNESS!!!!

Think! Think! Should I tell Miss Laura? I already told the teacher on him once today, and it made things worse.

I stood up and loudly said so everyone could hear me.

I grabbed my tray
and emptied it.
I was so angry. I
needed to have
some type of fun
after this fiasco.

I had my mind
on the prize: the
yellow-handle jump ropes.
This could still be an okay day.

The jump rope would make it all better.

Once outside, I could see the jump ropes and I ran over to them. My eyes were still wet with tears. But as I ran the wind dried them and blew away my sadness. I had been "eeewhhhhhhed" by my new classmates because of Delvin's lies.

The yellow-handle ropes were there, and as I grabbed them I felt so good. I jumped the entire recess. I jumped my problems and tears away all by myself.

As we lined up to return to class, Delvin stepped out of the line and smiled and said, "Raven let me kiss her and touch her butt."

This guy does not quit. It was round two and I wasn't even trying to fight back. I realized he had a mission to destroy my happy day.

I had nothing in me to say. Even if I had, it would have been drowned with "she's nasty," "eeewhhhhhh" and "gross" from my classmates.

Tears were no longer an option. I was fed up with this kid. I knew what to do. I needed my secret weapon – my mom.

As soon as I saw Miss Laura, I teared up and with a knot in my throat said, "Miss Laura, I feel sick, may I go to the nurse?"

Maybe I should tell Miss Laura first.

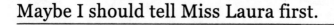

But I needed my mom now. $\longrightarrow$
I mean I really needed her now.

As soon as we got back to the classroom my teacher wrote me a pass to go to the nurse. She had a classmate go with me to show me the way to the nurse's office. I had never been to the nurse's office before and the school is really big.

There are two floors and a basement. My old school only had one floor and everyone knew everyone. This school is really big compared to my old school.

The girl who guided me to the nurse is a quiet girl. Her name is Fiona.

As we walked to the nurse's office, Fiona said, "You are sick of Delvin too?"

I nodded my head. "Yes."

I didn't want to talk. I was trying to prepare myself for the act I was going to give to the nurse. I had to concentrate and get ready for my performance.

I was a little bit afraid, but when I thought about my mom and dad and what they taught me about standing up for myself, I was not so scared of him anymore.

Fiona was a sweet girl. I hadn't really gotten a chance to get to know her. She continued to talk.

It is true, no one speaks to her, and when people do, they really do call her Funky Fiona, or they make fart noises to get her attention. She said she didn't tell anyone. Not her mom or dad.

Not even her teacher. She says she can't stand coming to school because of him and the way the other kids treat her. She says that's what Delvin does. If you cross him he will get you back.

Finally, we reached the nurse's office. As Fiona walked away to return to class I prepared myself for **SHOWTIME?** .

I walked into the office. I immediately clenched my stomach and teared up before the nurse could ask what was wrong.

I mumbled, "My tummy hurts so bad."

All LIES, but I needed my mom and couldn't tell anyone the truth until I felt completely safe.

The nurse made me lie down on the bed. She covered me up. Then she called my mom, who said she was on her way. I let out a deep sign of relief. Mom was coming to the rescue just as planned.

I stayed quietly on the bed in the nurse's office waiting for my mom to pick me up.

Tears rolled down my face onto the pillow. All these questions came into my head.

The next thing I heard was my mother's voice. It sounded so warm. It made me whimper and really cry out loud. The tears came on full force.

"My beloved daughter — what's wrong? Momma is here, sweetie."

It was like I was holding my breath, and finally with her arrival, I could breathe. I was safe.

I didn't even manage to get out of the bed before she rushed over and picked me up and cuddled me.

Man, I love this lady right now. She will protect me.

Finally we were in the car and I felt able to tell her what really went down. I took a deep, deep inhale and exhale and in one breath everything that happened flooded out.

I collected all my stuff from the classroom like nothing happened. Finally we were in the car and I felt able to tell her what really went down.

There was a pause.

More tears.

Hiccups.

What the heck is happening to me?

Maybe my hiccups triggered her transformation from a regular human mom into **Diva Mom** with super-powers.

During that pause I could almost see my mom transform into **Diva Mom**. Her face got tense and her eyebrows formed a frown on her face. It seemed like her teeth were clenched together. Her face looked beet-red. She was steaming HOT!

> Diva Mom emailed the superintendent, counselor, teacher, and prinicpal in one big email, then grabbed my hand and we walked back in to the school.

Suddenly, **Diva Mom** grabbed her cell phone. She emailed the superintendent, counselor, teacher and principal all in one email.

Then she marched back into the school dragging me behind her.

The counselor, Mr. Baker, was our first stop. She walked into his office and made me sit and tell him the entire story. I used my tears as proof of harassment and bullying.

Oh my gosh. She used the **S-WORD**. She said that I was ***SEXUALLY HARASSED AND BULLIED,***

Mr. Baker says he has tried to change this policy because there is a need for the kids to understand the **DOS aND DON'ts** rules in regard to their bodies.

Wait, there are rules???? If everyone knew the rules, then *maybe*, just *maybe* it would have prevented this **CRAY, CRAY** today.

Mom seemed somewhat satisfied with his response.

I think she understood that he has done all he can do and it's not up to him.

Before she power-walked out of the office, she told Mr. Baker that it was time to make a change to that policy and teach these children what they can and can't say to one another, regardless of their age.

Next, **Diva Mom** went straight to the principal. She told the story again, but this time with a stern suggestion for a policy change.

In the path of the storm was Mrs. Ross, the principal. We stopped by her office and Mom firmly spoke. Mrs. Ross listened and apologized for the events. She was calm but looked like she was a bit annoyed by our presence.

Diva Mom held her stance and was not backing down. She looked like a buffalo or lion.

Mrs. Ross said this is an issue that must be taken up with the superintendent.

Diva Mom firmly grabbed my hand to depart and said, "Thank you for providing an emotionally safe place for my daughter to learn and grow."

Wait. I *didn't* feel safe. *Did I miss something?*

Why did she say thank you to her when she didn't deserve it?

Oh, is that what adults call **SARCASM?** It's when someone says something completely the opposite of what they actually mean as a sort of joke.

Diva Mom was turned all the way up. I think that was her way of getting SASSY with Mrs. Ross.

That is when I knew **Diva Mom** was on 10 and completely enraged.

She gestured for me to continue on out the door, and I could not help but look back to try and see what was going on.

Was **Diva Mom** going to do something CRAZY?

Eventually we were in the car and the school was behind us.

Mom made a phone call as we drove home.

"Hello, I would like to make an urgent appointment to speak with the School Board Head, Dr. Lee, regarding sexual harassment and bullying of my second grader, Raven Hunter."
"Thank you, that time will do just perfectly."

As we drove we pulled into the parking lot of our favorite ice creamery.

YAAAAH, I screamed silently inside my head. All I could think of was sprinkles, sprinkles, sprinkles, sprinkles and more sprinkles. This place is the best. They have a small playground in the yard.

I grabbed my ice cream and ran to the swings.

What was I running for? No one else was here. Everyone was at school. Smiles.

Mom looked like she was still **Diva Mom**. She was still on the phone. I couldn't tell who she was talking to. I really didn't care right then. I was enjoying the sprinkles on my ice cream and the swing.

I wondered if I got closer to **Diva Mom** would I have heard her say a curse word?

#!%@*$

I look forward to hearing those words. It is so funny to see grown ups mess up, look embarrassed and apologize to us kids. My parents don't do much cursing, so when it happens, it's really exciting. **OH, BOY!**

Sometimes I can feel it coming just by listening to the tone of their voices.

Diva Mom was no longer on the phone. When I looked at her face she looked like a little hurt kitten. She was sad. She came over to me and sat beside me on the swing.

She looked like she was changing form, from superhuman **Diva Mom** to regular Mom, because she turned to me with tears in her eyes and said:

"Beloved, I am so sorry you experienced this. You are a strong, young person and you did the right thing to tell me and stand up for yourself. I am proud of you and I will fix this. I promise."

Mom then came in close for a deep hug. Hugs feel so good. And we headed home.

Wonder what tomorrow will be like.

OXO

XO

OXO

Chapter Eleven

HOMESCHOOL HORRORS

This week has been amazing and it is only Wednesday. Who says Wednesdays are not good? I like Wednesdays. At least, I like them now.

Mom has been on the phone a whole lot. She is using her professional voice, so I bet she is talking to school people about fixing the issue or about getting me into a new school. I can't quite tell, because she goes outside or into a different room away from me.

But I can tell she is frustrated, because when she returns she is not the same smiley-faced Mom. It's like she doesn't take enough time to transform back from **Diva Mom** to my regular mom.

It's not hard to notice how extra sweet my parents are being to me. Mom and Dad are super-ouper-duper nice to me. They let me watch PBS and Disney with no morning studying.

Mom begins to speak with slight hesitation in her voice.

"Beloved, you are a brave little person and I want to honor you. You should never experience disrespect and insult at school or anywhere, especially at this age," she says.

Everything she says is okay because I really, really like this new life.

I am off from public school while everyone else is in class because my parents snatched me out, all because Delvin was a meanie. I heard from Mom that Delvin was removed from Miss Laura's class. He spends his days with the teacher that helps kids with behavior problems. I remember passing that classroom. The teacher was a tough, mean guy who never smiled.

Those kids never got a lot of freedom. They were always in that little room. It was like a jail. I guess that's just the price you pay when you do mean things.

Mom says the principal and the superintendent did not handle the issue very well and did not take it seriously. I don't know the full details of all that went down, but I do know Mom was on the phone with Grandma Val and was UPSET. She said she was going to make the best of all of this. But how? I wonder.

Next Morning...

Wow! What time is it? I had the best dream last night. I was playing in a real-life Candy Land with all my favorite candies — cotton candy, sour straws, Now & Laters, Laffy Taffy, Milk Duds, Swedish Fish, and popcorn. Then I woke up. I *love* when I have great dreams like this.

My clock is hanging on the wall and reads 10:13. School has started already so I figure today is another day at home. YES!

I do my usual routine and brush my teeth, tongue and gums. I swish my mouthwash around.

Sometimes I want to swallow it because it is bubblegum flavored. It's not the best idea for me to have it because it is way too tempting. Dad says that swallowing mouthwash will make me sick, so I have only swallowed small amounts.

I wash my face and clean inside my ears. I put lotion on my face. I feel like lying back down for a few minutes. This bed feels the best.

I can't get back to sleep, but I will gaze out my window. My window gazing is disturbed by HAMMERING, DRILLING AND SAWING.

It is sort of odd because the **DO-IT-ALL DAD** usually does his projects on the weekend. I wonder what Dad is making?

Before I can think too long about the noise and my plans for the day, I get these *wonderful, amazing* smells coming from the kitchen. My legs automatically carry me towards the yummy food smells.

Mom greets me, "Good morning, sunshine."

I say, "Morning, Mom." I give her a hug because I am happy. No school, sleeping in and to top it off all this food looks like it wants to be in my tummy.

Mom says, "Come sit and eat. Dad and I have a surprise for you."

I sit and arrange my plate with bacon, pancake balls, potatoes and honeydew melon cubes, and I pour a big glass of orange juice. Wait, are those eggs over there? I will have some of those too.

I ask, "What's the surprise, Mom?"

As I dig into the most delicious breakfast in the world, I wait to hear about my surprise. Whatever it is, they have my attention.

Dad finally comes in and he goes to the sink and washes his hands. Mom says, "Great! We can tell you the surprise. Dad is building you a schoolroom in the basement.

"You are going to go to school right here. It is a homeschool, and I am going to be your new teacher."

I ask, "What is a homeschool and why is it in my basement?"

The basement was a wide and open play area for cartwheels and flips on the carpet. It had a huge television and comfy couches. Why would Dad make any changes to it?

I mean, is this what I have been doing, home-schooling? Are the yummy meals, television and waking up late part of homeschooling?

Dad announces, "It's all done, so we can go look at the room. Tell me what you think. Your mom let me design the space."

As we walk down to the new schoolroom in the basement, Mom tries to explain homeschooling.

"Homeschool is when you stay home and do all your lessons in your house instead of going to a school. You do the same work, you just do all your learning at home."

Thanks to that no-good Delvin's disrespectful-
ness, I have to leave my big-kid school just when
I was getting to like it. I will admit, the other kids
were a little rowdy, but I think I would have been
able to keep getting gold stars.

I'm special, my mom said so. She said I could
do anything.

I suppose my options are to go to a school with
that meanie who makes me cry or homeschool
with my mom.

I really don't want to go back to that school. I am
sort of embarrassed and upset at the school...
Still not completely sure I will like homeschooling. I need more information.

DECISIONS DECISIONS DECISIONS

When my mom used to volunteer to read and
help out in my first grade class at my old school,
she was *fun.* So would it be like that? Will other
kids be attending homeschooling with me?

I am going to have to think about this home-schooling thing. Mom is my *favorite* person but I really like being away from home from time to time. Would this mean I would be stuck at home all day with my mom, Gizmo and Caesar?

Hmmm, this might not be so bad.

Oh well. Before I completely reject this entire idea and SPAZZ out — I'd work my tears on Dad first and then give Mom my silent treatment — I need to head back to my happy place and go back to the kitchen and finish my breakfast.

I wonder how long I will be homeschooled? Just this week or for a whole year? Till the end of second grade?

I wonder what this will be like? Am I going to miss out on a bunch of fun field trips with my schoolmates?

This homeschool thing must be intense because Mom actually cooked my favorite — TURKEY BACON. ♥ ☆

She hasn't cooked meat in weeks. She has been trying this vegetarian thing on us. We don't eat real meat any more. When we have vegetarian meals I really don't eat much, I practically starve, but today I am eating. Eating it all.

Meat is yummy. YUM!

Maybe if I go with the homeschool thing, the meat will keep coming. I miss meat.

I keep asking if we can go back to eating real meat. Turkey bacon is my favorite. But Mom and Dad always, always buy the vegan bacon made from soybean.

Chapter Twelve

THE VEGETARIAN LIFE

Vegetarian just means you don't eat animals. Vegan is even worse — no meat or anything that comes from an animal. That means no cheese and no ice cream. That includes all the yummy foods like my favorites — macaroni and cheese, lasagna and pizza. Lucky for me, we are not doing vegan.

I hate tofu. Who invented tofu and why?

Imagine what dinner would be like if all those juicy burgers and yummy honey-glazed wings that you get at the drive-through and your favorite restaurant, or that grandma makes, were replaced with tofu, soy and vegetables?

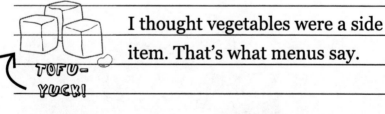

TOFU-
YUCK!

I thought vegetables were a side item. That's what menus say.

Side items: corn, broccoli and potatoes.

Menu

How can side items make a full meal? How can this be forced onto a child like me? Is there a law that prevents this? Maybe.

This new wave of no meat has taken over my house. I never even saw this coming.

Well there were a few episodes that I can recall.

There was the episode of Mom waking up in bed gagging because Dad was passing toxic gas in his sleep. She says  she woke up choking on the horrible smells that his body produced because it was trying to digest a bunch of meat. Mom says that too much  meat is hard on our digestive systems and puts a strain on our bodies. Not sure how true that is. I just know meat is *delicious*. ♥

I will say that when we don't eat meat, my poop doesn't smell. So maybe she is onto something. The worst is when we go out to eat. As soon as we sit down at the booth the server gives us menus.

"I feel so much lighter since we changed our diet up," Dad says while everyone looks at the menu.

Mom shows me the vegetarian options. It is all pretty much salad, meatless pasta and vegetable side dishes.

I thought side dishes were meant as a side dish, not the main meal. I don't get this, and I don't like it.

It's horrible to feel your mouth fill with saliva over food you can't have. I couldn't resist watching a waiter bring a plate of chicken wings and fries to a table near us.

I held up my menu a bit higher so Mom couldn't see my eyes. I pretended to be reading the menu, but I really needed to catch a better look at those wings. I could almost taste them. The worst part was when I found drool rushing towards my mouth.

Eating my favorite foods is a rare treat now. Since Mom is doing the VEGETARIAN THING, I look forward to going places just for the food.

Like tomorrow, I'm going to Justin's birthday party...

Justin is an okay kid. He lives on my street but he seems sort of strange to me. He is a collector of all things. I mean this kid collects leaves, rubber bands, pocket lint, rocks and bubblegum wrappers. It doesn't end. He collects everything and anything.

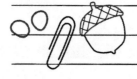

Once I overheard my mom on the phone with his mom and they were talking about his latest collection of old gum from public restaurants. He labels it and keeps it in a glass jar. Gross!

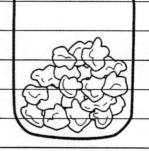

So, I'm looking forward to seeing Justin because — guess what? They eat meat. YIPPEE!

I am so excited.

I am going to have a hot dog as well as a burger.

I am going to eat lots of meat because I don't know when I will get more.

Mom will never know.
She will walk me to their house and leave or she will just watch me walk to their house. Either way she trusts that I will not eat meat because that's what she wants for me.

BUT I WANT MEAT.

I can hardly wait. Maybe I can go early? Wonder if they need help to set up? I am a great helper. I could stuff a few chicken wings in my mouth before the party gets started.

Birthday parties are few and far between. There are only a few kids my age on my street, and I don't have a bunch of friends.

I need to find more ways to visit houses where people eat meat. I feel like I am even losing weight, and I am already tiny.

I NEED MEAT!

I'll phone my Grandma Val and tell
her I want to visit her every weekend
and spend quality time with her. She will
definitely say yes because old people are lonely
and they are always happy to have company.

I love her a ton, but the real bonus of being
around Grandma Val is that she cooks meat.

Grandma Val is so cool. We have the best time
ever. We sing, dance, garden, watch movies, go
through old stuff, laugh and let's not forget we
cook. Not just any food — meat.

She calls herself a hip-hop
grandma because she knows a few slang words
that kids use — like *bling bling* (diamond jewelry),
on **fleek** (awesome) and **floss** (to show off).

Grandma Val keeps me entertained for sure.
I rarely use slang. I am still trying to understand
the English language.

Grandma Val has lots of cats. They have the funniest names. There is Big Boy, Grey Boy, Pretty Girl, Sheba and some others I don't remember.

The best part is her cats are allowed to hang out outside and come home when they want. The downside is that sometimes the cats kill a bird and try to bring it in the house.

When this happens Grandma Val squeals loudly and takes the bird away from the cat. She says, "Not in my house."

See, even the cats eat meat.

Grandma Val and I have fun together. And oh, boy, can she cook! She does not understand why eating meat is such a bad thing to do.

When she found out that our family was trying this vegetarian thing, she said loud and clear to my mom, "Honey, not I. Go ahead and starve yourselves."

Grandma Val says she has no regard for this meatless journey.

I look forward to visiting my grandma. I love her so much and I really, really, really want the meat.

Every time I go there she makes me the most *delicious* meals and she keeps giving me seconds. She says that I need my protein and iron.

I think she feels bad about the food at my house. After visiting Grandma Val, I always get a tummy ache the next day. I always eat too much because everything is so yummy.

One time, when my tummy hurt real bad, and
I could not tell Mom because she would be
suspicious, I called Grandma Val. She told me
to drink lots of prune juice.

I ran to the kitchen to get my cure. Grandma said
it would make me poop and flush the meat right
out of my system.

I didn't like the sound of that. All I knew is that
I needed to get rid of the meat before we left for
ballet that evening. I had never had prune juice
before. I hoped it tasted good.

Grandma says my little body is not used to
processing meat because I don't eat it anymore.

I rushed off to the kitchen.

Mom was in there on the phone. I tapped
Mom and asked, "Do we have prune juice?"

She said, "Yes, sweetie," and she poured me some.

Mom beamed with pride because I asked for a healthy drink.

Mom said, "Are you almost ready for ballet class?"

I was gulping down my drink. Taking a breath, I said yes and then went to get myself together for ballet class.

I thought my stomach started to feel a little better. On our way to class I noticed my stomach settling even more. Grandma is always right. She is so *smart.*

As soon as I got to class I tried to do the warm up, but I didn't feel too good. I raised my hand and asked the teacher if I could go to the restroom.

I ran past Mom, who was on her laptop, on my way to the restroom. I was worried because I knew if I took too long, Mom would come to see what was going on.

But I felt bad and just hoped this would be over fast.

Suddenly my stomach was OUT OF CONTROL. Maybe I overdid it with the meat, or could it be that prune juice?

I don't know how long I was on the toilet, but it must have been the whole class.

Then I heard heels — click-clack, click-clack.

The person stood still for a minute and then sprayed some air freshener in the restroom. How odd? Who does that?

"Honey, are you okay? Is your tummy upset?"

It was my mom. She was the click-clacker and air freshener sprayer.

I replied, "Yes, Mom. I feel horrible. Can we go home?"

She said, "Sure thing."

We collected our things and headed home. The entire ride home Mom grilled me and asked me a million questions.

"What do you think made your tummy upset?"

"What was the last thing you ate?"

There were too many questions coming at me. Mom is very familiar with the smells of meat-eater's poop. It is the reason our family stopped eating meat.

There were too many times when Mom was forced to smell horrid meat-eater's poop. I know she knows the smell really well.

One time she allowed Dad to use the restroom while she was taking a *bubble bath*. It smelled so bad she got out of her bath water. That really must have been a *DOOZY*.

Mom got so fed up with everyone's farts and poop smelling horrible she decided that our family wouldn't eat any more meat.

Now we all smell like fresh flowers. At least that's what she says. She is very happy about it too.

She just changed our diet without a warning or our permission, all because she is the Mom.

Have you ever eaten a complete meal that was only vegetables? It is tasteless.

Sometimes Mom buys fake meat and it taste like paper. Imagine eating that every day. I wonder if she thinks this food is delicious?

Grandma thinks I am not getting all the protein and vitamins I need because I don't eat a lot any more. I have to be really, really hungry to eat the fake meat.

Chapter Thirteen

THE
LAST SUPPER

It's my weekend with Grandma Val, and I am so happy. I can escape this veggie nightmare for a while.

I won't overdo it this time. Well, I will try not to. I just can't help myself when the meat is so well prepared.

As soon as I got to Grandma's she gave me an apron. We were going to grill ribs, burgers, hot dogs and corn. The corn goes on the side. That is where a vegetable should be.

When the food was all done, we arranged it so it looked *pretty* on a huge platter. We were ready to sit down and watch our movies.

But before I could get completely comfortable, the doorbell rang. I didn't know if Grandma heard it, because she was outside in the backyard, still cleaning up stuff.

I am not allowed to answer the door. So I sat
and waited.

Maybe she heard it. She usually hears everything
you don't want her to hear.

Mom and Dad must have smelled
that delicious barbecue, because
shortly after the doorbell rang I saw
them come through the backyard,
where Grandma was.

"Why hello, Mom," said Mom to her mom.

"BUSTED," Mom yelled so loud you would think
she had a bullhorn. "I have a mom who gives my
daughter meat against my will."

Next thing, Mom followed
Grandma into the TV room.
Dad stayed out in the yard. At a glimpse
he looked like he was doing his usual inspection
of things to fix.

Grandma Val chuckled and explained, "My grandbaby needs more protein and iron."

She even added, "Have you tasted those veggie dishes you make for your family?"

OUCH. Grandma was telling the truth. Mom's dishes are not delicious at all. And how do you just force your family to stop eating meat?

I told Grandma all about our food. She even stopped by a few times to taste it for herself. So she knows all about these veggie dishes. Mostly thumbs down.

Mom walked out to the backyard and continued her bullhorn chant so that all the neighbors could hear.

Grandma Val said, "Okay, okay, no more meat for Raven."

She winked at me to let me know she would keep making me meat.

Mom said, "If you can't follow house rules away from home, you won't leave home."

Grandma said, "Wait! How about easing every-one into this?"

"Maybe start off with no beef and pork, but do eat chicken and fish? And then slowly eliminate the chicken, then the fish."

I smiled from ear to ear.

All the time I could hear some rumbling and hammering coming from the yard. Dad was fixing something on the patio in the background.

Dad was smart to stay out of this.
I wondered if he needed any help?

Dad did seem very distracted when he arrived.

Like Mom, he was on a mission — just not the exact same one.

He found something to fix, a wiggly shelf on Grandma's garden table outside.

He always carries his tools in the trunk just in case he gets a chance to fix something. He lives for these moments — to fix stuff.

Usually, all he needs is his **DO-IT-ALL** utility knife. Mom and I got it for him for Father's Day. It's pretty neat. It's a wooden knife and it has all these cool tools on it, like a screwdriver, file, knife, ruler and some other stuff.

He won't let me play with it because he says that I might hurt myself and it's for adults ONLY.

Even if I wanted to play with it, which sometimes I do, I couldn't because he keeps it attached to his keys on his belt loop.

Usually, all Dad needs is his *DO-IT-ALL* utility knife. It has all these cool tools on it.

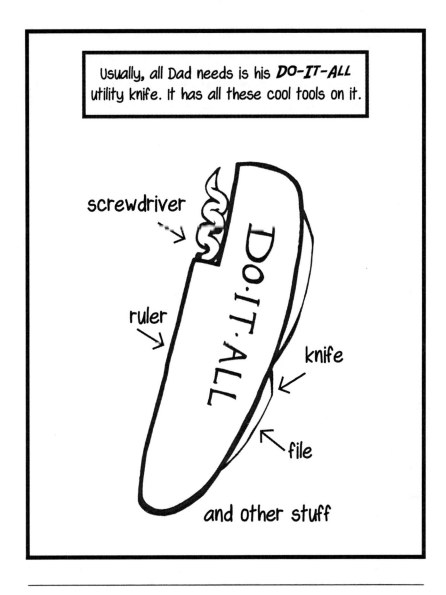

screwdriver

ruler

DO·IT·ALL

knife

file

and other stuff

Dad found something to fix, a wiggly shelf on Grandma's garden table outside.
He always carries his tools in the trunk just in case he gets a chance to fix something.

Then Mom brought in some of her already-prepared veggie dishes for everyone to eat.

We all sat down around the television. Mom pushed the meat dishes to the side and placed her dishes in front of us.

"Dig in," she said with a smirk. It was almost like she knew they were not tasty.

Grandma Val replied, "How about a little salmon and chicken for everyone?"

Suddenly Mom popped in the movie *What Are You Eating?* as everyone began to dig into this feast and the sides Mom brought. SNIFF SNIFF

Within the first ten minutes of the show we all are tearing up and crying. Grandma and me stopped eating our meat and started to eat the vegetables.

Everyone was crying about the treatment of the poor animals. I noticed we were all passing the big bowl of vegetable pasta around and not eating the meat.

Grandma Val mumbled, "Just sad."

Mom said, "This is another big reason why I don't want us to eat meat. Look at how the big farms and animal factories mistreat the animals."

Of course we all cried. We all love animals.

The documentary was teary and sad. I couldn't watch it much. They were just plain mean to the chickens, cows and pigs. I mean, why would they do that?

Mom said, "It's all about money. Not eating meat is one way we can make them stop. If we don't buy it, they will stop selling it."

She said, "Soon, if enough people stop eating so much meat, the farmers and butchers will stop killing so many animals."

Thankfully, Grandma turned off the TV. It was too much for her. It had been too much for me.

We couldn't get through twenty minutes of the show.

Grandma made a *BIG ANNOUNCEMENT*. She proudly said, "I want to try this with you all."

All because she saw how bad they treat the animals we eat.

Grandma added, "Honey, we have to do some work on these vegetarian recipes you are feeding your family."

Everyone laughed.

When it was time to head off, grandma pulled me aside and apologized for encouraging me to disobey my mom. I just smiled and hugged her. On the drive home I secretly committed to stop eating meat. This time, I made up my own mind.

Of course, Mom and Dad tag-teamed me about living in secret disobedience. Blah, blah, blah, blah.

The only thing I have to do is give a head-nod now and again or say "yes, ma'am" or "yes, sir."

More blah, blah, blah.

The only thing I could think about was getting home to my animals. I understand killing animals for food, but why do they keep the animals in those conditions?

No free space and no place to have fun. When I get home, I'm taking Gizmo outside to roam a little bit.

Chapter Fourteen

SUMMER CAMP, PLEASE!

welcome!

I have been bugging Mom every chance I get about summer camp. I survived a full school year of homeschooling with **Diva Mom**, and now it's reward time.

I just need a break. Some time to do kid stuff without Mom or Dad around.

Anything to get out of the house and get to the recreation center's new pool park.

Our community recreation center has been teasing me. They've been building a full-on water park. Mom drives past it on the way to the grocery store. I've been watching them build it, like, forever.

It has this **MASSIVE** sign.

UNDER CONSTRUCTION

Well, guess what? Now it's all DONE.

Now when we drive past I feel a rush come over my body. It's sort of like that feeling you get just before you eat when you're starving. It's that. Whatever that is called.

Mom's been taking me to Splashers, a water park that has only one slide. She says that the fee for the new recreation center pool is ridiculously high. But we can plan a day to go there this summer.

Wait ... What ...

... A DAY... as in one day ... out of the entire summer ... ⟶

That just doesn't sound promising to me. I can hear doubt in her voice. She's not even *excited*.★

But I have a plan to get to the water park.

SUMMER CAMP.

So it is back to asking every day if she'll enroll me in summer camp. *Please?*

Of course I want to meet new people ... sort of ...

Yes, I want to learn how to sew, dress fashionably, cook and all that stuff ... kind of ... not really ...

Have you seen the new pool park?

O.M.G.

It's *crazy amazing*. It has three slides, a lazy river and a surf pool.

Lucky for me, the recreation center has a summer camp for girls and boys my age, and they let the day campers swim in the new pool park. Well, it's the only pool. So where do you think the summer campers will swim?

It has to be at the pool park!

Yes! I am trying something different. I really, really, really want to go to summer camp at the recreation center this year.

Most summers I hang out with my family and we do stuff together like camping, going to the pool, amusement parks and watching movies. I am okay with still doing all that, but I want to go to the new pool park too.

And since Mom won't pay the high price, going to summer camp is my best chance to get there. Sometimes a girl has to get creative!

YIPPEE! Mom enrolled me in day camp for two months. But I gotta pick which groups I want to join. Mom picked a few she likes — fashion design and cooking — and I get to pick the rest.

I don't know what to pick.

I suppose drawing is one choice.

And ...

AND ...

I have to hurry with my picks. Mom says the deadline to hold my spot is soon.

Chapter Fifteen

AT CAMP

Today was my first day at summer camp.

I cannot even believe that I was around so many older kids. Older kids are interesting because they always have DRAMA. Sometimes it is better than watching a movie.

There are teen and adult counselors at every turn so I feel very safe. Lindsey and Ben are my group's counselors. They are pretty young looking. I know they are both in high school and they can drive. They are nice so far.

I am in complete awe of the eleven- and twelve-year-old kids. They seem like real grown ups. They have cell phones and Instagram. I am not completely sure what Instagram is, but they have it.

I'll see these big kids first thing in the morning when they separate us into our groups. I try to follow them to find out what's going on but I cannot do it for long because we are in different groups.

Today, I just sat, stared and tried to listen for curse words and I tried to guess their pre-teen drama. #!%@*$

Honestly, I want just one thing from this camp — the POOL PARK!

Can you believe it? We'll get to play and go crazy at the waterpark pool three times a week. ♡

Mom thinks that I wanted to learn some new skills. She made me pick sessions on my own. There were so many options I felt dizzy.

They had sessions for junior lifeguards, writing, drawing, soccer, theater and so much more.

I didn't care what session I picked because I really just wanted the pool park with its swirly slide and lazy river. And to get some time away from home.

I couldn't pick my sessions because I really wasn't very interested. Camp is camp — as long as I could go to the pool park I just didn't care.

So I asked Dad to do the picking. But I did not really think about the consequences.

He picked chess camp. Not just once. He picked chess four times. That's twenty days of chess learning.

Chess is SUPER BORING. Go figure that.

YAWN...

So today I was sitting in chess camp waiting for our counselors Ben and Lindsey to tell us it's our group's turn for water fun. ♥

How were these other kids even focusing on learning anything about chess when there's a great, big, wondrous world of fun right outside the window.

Finally, our counselor brought in our chess instructor. He is a skinny, tall, hairy man. He has messy hair and he was wearing flip-flops. He stood at the front of the room as we sat at tables across from one another.

"Hi, chess lovers. My name is Mr. Parker. I will be your chess instructor for the next two hours, and every day for the next week."

The next two hours? Oh, my ... I did not know how I was going to get through this.

The counselors teamed me up with a little boy. He didn't speak to me, and I didn't speak to him either. We were just sitting with a chessboard between us waiting for instructions.

And I could hardly focus. *WOO HOO!*

I couldn't hear what the instructor

said. I just heard the muffled screams

of fun and splashes of water from the water park.

The instructor finally said, "Introduce yourself to

your chess mate sitting across from you."

My partner lifted his head, which was

resting on his hand, which was propped

up by his elbow that was on the table, and

he leaned forward to shake my hand, "Hello, my

name is Hero. I am eight years old."

I took his hand and lightly shook it and said, "Hi,

Hero, my name is *Raven*. I am eight too."

He laughed and said, "You are not eighty-two."

I laughed and thought this might be sort of fun

or something. I like clever jokes.

211

Finally, someone with smarts and funnies.

Now it was time to *show off* — at CHESS.

Okay, let's play then. I was all in.

There was no swimming today. I wanted to get to that pool. I did enjoy myself at chess and I am looking forward to going back tomorrow.

Plus tomorrow is a swim day. The counselor gave Dad a pool reminder notice when he picked me up today.

Strangely enough, I actually missed Mom and Dad and home today just a little. A tiny little bit.

More than anything, I am tired. I've been playing, moving and learning stuff since around nine this morning. I am pooped. This must be what being an adult feels like.

Tomorrow is going to be a *great day*!

Chapter Sixteen

DAY TWO OF CAMP

Today was another camp day. But because today was a swim day, it was going to be the _best day._

YAAAH!

Mom pulled my swim goggles out and placed them in a little backpack along with a swimsuit, beach towel, sunscreen, flip-flops, moisturizing body wash, lotion and a swim cap.

She laid my clothes out on the bed — tank top, undies with the words "Terrific Tuesday" printed on them and some cutoff shorts.

I got dressed and checked myself in the mirror. I looked _perfect_... my perfect. But then I thought, if I put my swimsuit on under my clothes, I'd be the quickest, and I'd be first into the pool.

"Raven, go eat breakfast. It's almost time to go," Dad muttered as he walked past my room on his way downstairs for breakfast.

I had no time. I hurried and pulled all my clothes off and somehow shuffled my swimsuit on. I threw on my shorts and tank top, grabbed my backpack and headed down to eat.

Mom had put out a huge fruit bowl with pine-apple, blueberries and watermelon. Watermelon is my *favorite* fruit. The melon was cut in huge cubes. I sat down and ate as much watermelon as I could. She gave me some buttered toast too.

Simply yummy... ♥

As I sat at the table munching, Mom rushed over to me with the hair box.

It was filled with moisturizers, gels, leave-in conditioners, rubber bands, ribbons, beads, bobby pins, ponytail holders and all types of combs and brushes.

She braided my hair and then gently patted me on the head to signal that she was finished and said, "All done. Now your pretty locks can fit under your swim cap."

Then she kissed me on the cheek and said, "Enjoy your day!"

I was so happy because I already knew it was going to be fun, so I said, "I will."

Before I walked out the door, Dad sprayed me with some stuff from a can. It tickled, so I squirmed each time he sprayed it. It was sunscreen so the sun wouldn't burn my skin.

When we got to the recreation center, I had a big smile on my face, and Dad signed me in.

He said goodbye with a hug and a kiss. I was ready!

All the kids were outside playing and running. Some kids were throwing a ball. Some were jumping rope. Some kids were sitting at a table. I didn't see Hero.

I walked towards the kids and then saw one of my counselors. She directed me to sit, explore or play.

I went to a picnic table where there was a whole bunch of kids. Some were sitting on the bench and others were on the table. I only saw girls at this table. There were eight- and nine-year-old girls and ten-, eleven-, twelve- and thirteen-year-old girls here. I saw them polishing each other's nails and braiding hair.

As soon as I sat down, one of the older girls said out loud, "You have *pretty* hair. Let me braid it."

Before I could answer, another older girl said, "You are cute, let me polish your nails." She held up a sparkly blue color and grabbed my hand."

I didn't know what to say. I just smiled and said, "Thank you."

In no time, my hair was re-braided and my nails were sparkly and in the air-dry cycle.

What did I get myself into?

Before I could completely settle into my discomfort the counselors blew their whistles. That's the signal to go find your group and line up with them.

I grabbed my backpack from my side and hopped up from the bench to run to my group. The chess group.

I watched everyone scramble to their groups as the counselors began to lead us inside, one group at a time.

I hung my backpack on a hook and realized that my chess mate was missing. I wondered what his deal was? Yesterday he was all about chess. Today he didn't even show up. Oh well.

I kind of hoped that he would be here. It was only day two. I had just gotten used to him as a partner and I really didn't want to meet anyone else. I wanted to get to know more about him.

He seemed weird to me. A GOOD WEIRD. Not the dangerous weird.

Lucky for me, today we watched a movie all about chess. Who knew people could talk about chess for so long?

No need to be polite. No need to pretend to listen to anyone and try to ignore their heavy breathing or nail biting or table tapping. This activity didn't call for a partner.

We all got a small bag of popcorn and
sat on the floor and watched the chess movie.

ZZZZZZZZ

I must have drifted off, because
suddenly I was woken by Mr. Parker's
voice saying, "And that's the history of chess."

Great! It was over.

You already know what came next!

SWIM SWIM SWIM
SWIM SWIM SWIM
SWIM SWIM SWIM.

I felt an intense rush and my body was
screaming ready.

I had to **number 1** (pee).

I mean really badly.

I don't know how I napped through the movie needing to go to the bathroom. I hadn't even drunk my bottle of water yet.

It was probably all the watermelon. I ate a whole lot.

It's my favorite. Of course I would eat a lot of it. I scurried over to Mr. Parker and asked to go to the restroom.

He said to hurry because the counselors would be here at any moment to take us all to the pool for swim time.

I hurried off to the girl's bathroom, unsnapping my shorts before I rushed into the stall. Oh, no. I couldn't pull down my undies.

OH MY GOODNESS...
SERIOUSLY...

I realized that I had on a full-body swimsuit.

I would have to undress completely.

I felt myself begin to hold back tears because I had to go — really 𝒢𝒪 — like right 𝕹𝕺𝖂. And all the fixings were right there — tissue and toilet.

My swimsuit was the hold up. Me and my bright ideas...I was so clever, putting on my swimsuit on under my clothes.

There was no time to panic. I had to lift my tank top up to my neck. Pull my swimsuit down over my shoulders. One at a time. And squat with my knees bent far enough apart to stop my shorts falling onto the germy floor.

Mom always tells me to wash my hands before and after I use the bathroom to stop the spread of germs from myself to everyone else, and from everyone else to me. And I normally do.

But this time I just couldn't handle the sound of running water. Running water would have just been asking for trouble.

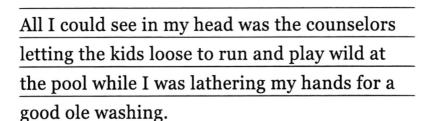

I nearly had a panic attack because time was so short. I had to get to the pool for swim time.

After I was done using the bathroom, I pulled my swimsuit back up as fast as I could. Put my arms through my tank. Snapped my shorts.

I needed more time ...

Then I had to wash my hands.

All I could see in my head was the counselors letting the kids loose to run and play wild at the pool while I was lathering my hands for a good ole washing.

Finally, I was all done. I walked back to the room to grab my backpack. But the group had

already gone to the pool. I went straight there.
I skipped the girl's locker room completely.
I mean, I was wearing my swimsuit already.

I put my backpack down and traded
my sneakers for flip-flops.

As I stuffed my shoes into my backpack, my
swim cap fell out. I'd almost forgotten it.

I tried to put my swim cap on
my head but the braid the older
girl did this morning had come
half undone and my hair was too big to fit. I
wished I still had the tight braid Mom did this
morning.

Oh, crap!

I walked up to Lindsey, one of the counselors,
and asked for help putting my swim cap on.
She tried hard to stuff my hair in the cap. She
called another counselor over to help. By this

time, one was holding my head steady as the other one was trying to pull the swim cap over my hair.

I wanted it done. I didn't care if they hurt my head. I was missing too much playtime.

As they stuffed my now completely unbraided hair into the swim cap, all I could think of was why did I let that girl touch my hair?

I didn't know how to say no to her. I was caught off guard. Plus they were cool and nice to me.

DEEP SIGH.

OH, WELL!

"Ouch," I said as the swim cap firmly snapped my forehead.

SNAP!

225

All I could hear were splashes, squalls, squeals and whistles. I could see kids having a complete blast.

I was the last kid there but it was okay because I was finally at the pool and I was going to have all sorts of water fun.

I almost ran, but I remembered we cannot run near the pool area. So I walked quickly to the pool and went straight for the slide.

I tried E-V-E-R-Y-T-H-I-N-G out!

The lazy river.
All the slides.
The water sprinkler.

YESSSSS!

This is what I live for.

If only I could have this in my backyard.

Before I knew it, the whistles were

blowing and it was time to get out of the pool.

I started to head towards my backpack. But I

could feel my heavy hair resting on my shoulders

and neck. Oops! My swim cap came off. I looked

for it, but I didn't see it.

SWIMMING CAP: MISSING IN ACTION

My group lined up to shower off. I was so keep-

ing my swimsuit on in the shower. I started to

organize my dry clothes and I couldn't believe

this was happening to ME... I couldn't find...

where are my...wait... oh no... I DIDN'T HAVE

ANY UNDIES!

Did I forget to stuff them in my bag

this morning when I put my swimsuit on under

my clothes?

I couldn't not wear underwear. It just wouldn't

be right. I would be so uncomfortable for the

rest of the day. Someone might notice!

People would know.

I would know.

Plus, I think it is illegal to not wear underwear in public.

I was nice and showered and as dry as I could get wearing a wet swimsuit. I looked in the mirror and got a glimpse of my hair.

WHAAAAAAAAA!!!!
THE WHAAAAAAA!!!

WHAAA
WHAAA HAPPENED?!

#CurlyGirl Issues

I looked like a troll doll.
I had never seen my hair like this, ever.

Mom always works magic and makes it soft and smooth.

Right then my hair was hard, frizzy and dry.

I had no brush or comb with me because the swim cap was supposed to keep my braided hair dry.

I went back inside with my group. I was freezing. It was my wet swimsuit. It didn't mix well with air conditioning. My swimsuit was making my dry clothes wet.

All I could do was hope I could go outside where it was hot to dry off and warm up.

An older boy chuckled at me and said, "If your hair looks like that after you swim, you should really not swim."

Huuuuh.

Tears welled up in my eyes. I wore my wet towel on my head to hide my hair for the rest of the afternoon.

Mom picked me up. She took a glance at me and asked, "What happened?"

I told her every single thing that happened. Even the no-underwear part. I just wanted to be ready before everyone else and be first into the pool.

The entire ride Mom looked like she was trying not to burst out laughing.

All this was so not funny though.

"I think it's time for me to make you an appointment with Ms. Tiffany J., my *beautician*. For now, I will show you a short and simple way to manage your hair. You will need to practice it a lot," Mom said.

After I got home, Mom washed and conditioned my hair in the sink. After she rinsed it out and towel dried it, she pulled out the hair-care box filled with all the magical products to make my hair beautiful again.

Mom walked me through each step. She told me it seems like a lot of work but it's necessary for our type of hair. #Curly Girl Issues

Hair Care Steps

1. Shampoo, shampoo, shampoo. Mom always uses her fingertips to gently scratch my scalp. She says it gets my scalp clean from even the tiniest dirt.

Shampoo, condition, comb carefully, rinse.

2. Then towel dry.

Towel dry.

3. Squirt moisturizer or leave-in conditioner in my hands. Rub both hands through my hair from root to ends (this takes some time).

4. When it is all soft, comb through starting at the ends slowly and gently. Comb further up and closer to the roots. Put more moisturizer or leave-in conditioner on the edges of my hair around my neckline and forehead.

5. *Styling Time!!*

Then she said I could put my hair in any style. I always choose *Curly Girl Afro*! For my curly girl look I have to put my damp hair in individual braids or twists and allow my hair to set or dry overnight. That's when the magic starts to occur. When we finally undo the braids or twists... VWAALAA... (voila!!) *My Curly Girl Hair.* ♥

Wowww ... I think I got it. Well. Sort of ...
It was pretty tough, and I will need a lot of
practice to do my hair well.

My hair is thick and curly. And it is going to take
a lot of energy to manage it.

Mom let me practice on my hair before she
braided it again.

She reminded me not to let people play with my
hair. Mom said little girls may not know what
they are doing and might pull your
hair out. And sharing other people's
combs and brushes is sharing germs.

Before I could even completely wonder how to tell
the older, cool girls that they can't play with my
hair, Mom said I could blame it on her and simply
say, "My mom won't let me," or, "I can't, I will get
in trouble with my mom."

She must have known what I was thinking.

Hmmmm… that works… let Mom be the bad guy.

I am okay with that. It beats the older cool girls getting upset with me. Let them get upset with Mom.

The next day when I woke up, Mom had me unravel my hair twists … it was like magic. I was back to my #CurlyGirlStatus.

My hair was back to being amazing. Mom reminded me that **All Great Things Take Time** and to be patient.

The entire drive to summer camp, I looked at my reflection in window. I smiled and smiled even more on the outside because I just like

everything about me. I am getting better and better. I am back to my normal pretty girl self and ready to brave and rave it.

I didn't see Hero on day three or on day four. I wondered if he was ever coming back to camp? He missed chess and pool time and a bunch of fun.

Finally, one day, I saw Hero near the check-in area going toward everyone else.

But he stopped and made a detour towards this huge tree. He sat down. I could tell Hero was sad because his head dropped low.

He just sat there against the tree.

I was unsure of what I should do. Should I go over to smile at him and say hello or allow him space to feel however he felt?

I decided to walk over to Hero only because he seemed really *cool and fun.*

I had no clue what to say. The closer I got the more I could tell that he was super sad.

I sat next to him where he leaned against the tree and said nothing.

I pulled my sketchbook out of my backpack and started to draw.

I felt really bad for him. I didn't know why he was so sad, but I didn't want him to feel that way around me.

I drew a picture of a king chess piece we had learned all about and wrote, "Hope you feel better. Your friend, Raven."

He looked at me and smiled. I could tell he was feeling a little better.

We watched as the older girls formed an assembly line to do all the younger campers' hair and nails.

We both chuckled at the sight.

The counselors all began to blow their whistles to round everyone up into their groups.

Hero got up while I put my sketchpad away. As he looked down at me, I said, "Can you give an eighty-two-year-old girl a hand?"

He reached out his hand and laughed. He said, "You remember?"

The day carried on and I never asked him what was wrong or anything.

Today I wasn't ready to go home. I actually enjoyed playing chess with Hero.

Hero was smiling and so was I.

I even hoped that Mom or Dad would be late, but that never happens. These two are like robots. They are always on time.

I asked Hero, "How did you get your name?"

He said his dad named him. He is a military Hero. He started to ramble about his dad being super awesome.

Then he said, "Sometimes being too awesome can be bad and everyone needs you. Like the military keeps needing my dad."

He added that his dad would soon be leaving again. He has to go out of the country for a long time on a military deployment.

I thought that sounded sort of cool, but apparently it is not. It's super dangerous. Soldiers die.

So now I understood why Hero was so sad.

He loved his dad and didn't want him to leave.

Understandable.

Hero's dad left during summer camp. He was far away now helping to protect America or something like that.

When summer camp was over Mom and Dad kept in touch with Hero's mom so that Hero and I could play often. Sometimes his mom would drop him off at our house.

I heard his mom tell my mom that he doesn't make friends very easily and how he gets bored with kids his own age. Guess I am not boring.

Our parents were excited that we both finally had a friend we enjoyed spending time with. We did a bunch of stuff together.

We even went camping, watched movies and played video games.

Hero is my *best friend.*

HE IS MY BESTIE.

And my first and only BESTIE!!!...

Chapter Seventeen
CLOSE CALL

WOW! That was a close call. **I found you!!!!**
My dearest diary, I almost lost you forever.
I HAVE MISSED YOU SOOOOO MUCH!!!!

I am so glad that I checked this box of books and toys before I let Dad give it away to the thrift store. Someone would have discovered all my secrets and stories.

Look. It's been years since I wrote here. So many memories you missed: birthdays, vacations and adventures.

Ooo... oooo. ...... I have even learned cursive. Watcha think?!

Let's catch up. I was homeschooled for second, third and fourth grade. You missed a lot of drama little friend. Now we are reunited, I promise I will keep you close.

But there isn't much room left so I'll have to get you a sister. ♡

A lot has changed. I am ten. I am going into the fifth grade and I am going to go to REAL school.

No more homeschooling for me. We are moving to a bigger house.

Mom can't homeschool me anymore because she is going to open a yoga studio.

YAAAH for me.

My new school is a private school that specializes in the arts and sciences. I had to audition, take a test and do an interview with the principal just to get accepted.

I will be a new kid at a new school again. I'm looking forward to being in a class with other kids. Being a homeschool kid is very lonely.

Don't tell Mom, but just between us, being with Mom all day really tested both of our patience.

Sometimes I really get annoyed being around her all day long.

I think you can understand. We were together day in and day out. We got no breaks from one another.

It is time for me to spread my wings and take the

SUPER HERO PRINCESS WARRIOR BRAVE RAVE

out into the world.

I am going to ask Mom to take me to the bookstore so I can buy another diary.

Gotta go!

ABOUT THE AUTHOR

Raquel Hunter is a real-life **Diva Mom**, so she is perfectly qualified to write the **BRAVE RAVE** book series. In fact, she's been seen writing this book wearing the cutest pink yoga pants and flip-flops that have more bling than the Queen of England's tiara.

More than anything else in the world, Raquel believes that little girls can grow up to do amazing things. After all, she joined the Navy when she was 17 years old and got to live in Japan during her four-year tour of duty. After that, she got a degree in social work and became a youth mentor. She has also designed purses and made candles.

These days, when she is not writing *Brave Rave* books or teaching yoga she is doing her most important job — being Raven's mom.

Raquel lives in St. Louis with her diva-in-training-daughter Raven and her husband, the *DO-IT-ALL DAD.*

Acknowledgements
My deepest gratitude goes out to everyone who has helped bring the *Brave Rave* book to life.

From my beautiful daughter Raven, who has allowed me to tell her stories, to my husband, who is my rock in so many more ways than I can express. I appreciate and love everyone who has been part of this journey, but I want to take this chance to recognize a few people who have made a very special contribution:

Janette Lonsdale of The Red Stairs (Editor & more)
You graciously guided me through all the twists and turns of turning the *Brave Rave* story into a book. You introduced me to creative professionals whose talents were the magical fairy dust that turned my ideas into reality. Your knowledge and continued support have been priceless.

Eve Drueke (Artistic Book Designer)
From your excitement for the story to your enthusiasm, to your boundless imagination, you have inspired me. You put the icing and the sprinkles on this book. Your creativity is unmatched.

Aubrey Berkholtz (Illustrator)
You listened to our family stories, studied our family photos and with a few deft strokes of your pencil, created the beautiful drawings that are such an important part of the Brave Rave. Your illustrations are perfect in every way.

Peggy Nehmen (Book Designer & more)
Your attention to detail and commitment to excellence make you a true professional. You answered all 25 of my daily phone calls and emails without complaint. Your attentive work and your expert guidance have made this book everything I dreamed it could be.

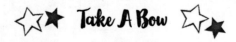

Keep reading Brave Rave series and meet my forever besties

Coming soon!

Superhero
book series

Mighty Lovely
book series

Visit **BraveRaveBook.com** to find out more
about each book series' release date
and get fabulous, super cool goodies:
The *Brave Rave* journal, **Diva Mom** coffee mug,
the **DO-IT-ALL-DAD** utility keychain,
posters, pencils, bookmarks and lots more.

Puzzle answer:

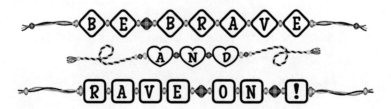

BE BRAVE AND RAVE ON!

Make a bookmark!

Keep Reading,
Keep Writing!

Brave
Rave